with
Reading

Sir Scatterbrain, the Hopeless Knight

By Stéphane Daniel

Illustrated by Christophe Besse

FRANKLIN WATTS
LONDON•SYDNEY

Meet the Scatterbrains

Tom Scatterbrain

King Humphrey

Queen Mary

Princess Rose

CHAPTER 1
The Knight's Quest

Sir Tom Scatterbrain was about to start his quest for a princess. He said farewell to his father, King Humphrey, and his mother, Queen Mary.

Then he went to find his beloved nanny, Miss Jocelyn. She was in the keep with her feather duster, trying to hide her sadness.

"Goodbye, Nanny!" waved Sir Scatterbrain. "Goodbye, Tom, my dear boy," she replied. "Keep safe!"

"There's nothing to worry about," Tom Scatterbrain said, lifting his sword from its scabbard. "With this sword to protect me, I have nothing to fear."

"Look after yourself," Miss Jocelyn said, turning away to hide her tears.

For centuries, the Scatterbrains had been born and raised in Luckless Castle. When the time came, they set off on a journey around the world to find their princess.

Tom's father, King Humphrey, had freed
Tom's mother, Mary, from the clutches of
an almighty giant. Before that, his
grandfather, King Edward, had saved
his wife, Princess Maerwynn, from an
evil sorceress.

Tom was sure that he would
make the Scatterbrains proud.
But he couldn't help
feeling nervous
when he crossed
the castle
drawbridge.

He knew nothing about life outside Luckless Castle. As he reached the edge of the kingdom, he looked back. The castle looked like a tiny dot in the distance.

CHAPTER 2
The Princess and the Dragon

The first few days of Sir Scatterbrain's quest were full of fun. He stopped at many villages and visited plenty of new kingdoms! But he quickly realised that freeing a princess wasn't going to be easy.

First of all, *there needs to be a princess.*

Second of all, there needs to be a princess *in danger.* And finally, he needs to get to the princess *before* the other knights do – and he had seen many knights on his way! Eventually he reached a tiny fishing village beside an immense lake.

He discovered that a princess called Arabella had travelled to the island in the middle of the lake but had never come back.

"Why didn't she return?" he asked the captain of the biggest boat. "Can't the princess swim?"

"She can, but she can't fight the very ferocious dragon who lives there!" he replied.

Sir Scatterbrain didn't waste a second.

"Captain, will you bring me closer to the island? I'll fight your little beastie!"

Soon Sir Scatterbrain was at the bow of the boat. He hadn't seen the knight in a small boat heading in the same direction.

"I can't go any further – there's a reef in the way," the captain announced, dropping the anchor.

"Never mind, I'll swim from here!" Sir Scatterbrain replied, ready to show his courage. He stepped to the side of the boat and took a very deep breath.

The captain rushed forward. "Wait! Don't you think you'd better…?"

But it was too late – Sir Scatterbrain jumped into the water … and sank.

Luckily, as he neared the bottom of the lake, he saw a net. He grabbed hold of it and pulled himself back to the surface. The captain and his men lifted Scatterbrain out of the water.

"You didn't let me finish," said the captain. "I was going to say that you should take your heavy armour off before you jump!"

"Oh dear, I didn't think of that!" the knight admitted. Suddenly he spotted a rival knight, Sir Fightalot, in a boat across the lake and realised that he had lost this quest!

Sir Fightalot slew the dragon and freed the Princess Arabella, who promptly fell madly in love with her handsome rescuer.

Not ready to give up, Scatterbrain set off again, convinced that there were plenty of other princesses to save in the world.

CHAPTER 3
The Crossroads

It was exactly three months since Sir Tom Scatterbrain had left Luckless Castle. As he approached the next village, there was an eerie atmosphere. The streets were empty, the doors were shut and the windows were all boarded up.

Sir Scatterbrain was looking for a blacksmith for his horse. Finally he found one, but he had to knock on the door many times before the blacksmith dared to open it.

"What's up with you, my good chap?" Scatterbrain asked.

"You must be a stranger!" gasped the blacksmith. "Haven't you ever heard of Ironmouth the Giant?"

"No, who is he?"asked Sir Scatterbrain.

"He's a brute who has been terrifying us for years. Every time it's a full moon he comes from his forest to steal from us, destroying everything in his way! And it's a full moon tonight!"

"I see," stammered Scatterbrain.

"Does the giant have a princess as a prisoner by any chance?"

"Not that I know of," replied the blacksmith.

"Just a word of advice, brave knight," the blacksmith continued. "When you leave the village, you will reach a lime tree where the path divides. Do not take the right path or it will lead you straight to Ironmouth's forest. Remember to turn left at the lime tree."

Sir Scatterbrain climbed back on his horse and swiftly left the village. Soon he arrived at a huge lime tree where the path divided into two.

"Now, what did the blacksmith tell me? I must take the right path after the lime tree. Yes, I'm sure he said take a right turn." Sir Scatterbrain rode on, but the path became darker and darker. Soon he was in a very deep, dark forest. Rocked by the motion of his horse, Scatterbrain started to feel sleepy. He stopped at a beautiful spot alongside a stream, climbed down from his horse and saw the entrance to a cave.

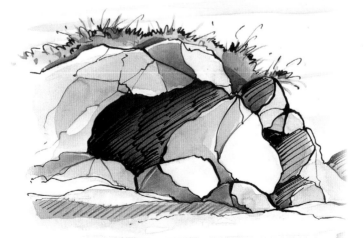

He couldn't resist the soft bed of moss in its entrance. He lay down and immediately fell into a deep sleep.

CHAPTER 4
Giant Trouble!

The sound of loud voices from a
passageway suddenly woke Sir Scatterbrain
up. He decided to crawl inside to see where
it led. A few minutes later, the passage
opened up into a much, much bigger cave.

In front of him two gigantic creatures were busy arguing. Scatterbrain had crawled straight into Ironmouth the Giant's lair! "You have to," the big giant told his son. "We have all had to do it!"

"But Dad…"

"No, you are old enough to carry out your giant responsibilities. At your age, I had already kidnapped two princesses!"

"Two?" Little Giant asked.

"Yes, two! So you are perfectly capable of capturing one!" his dad told him.

"But I don't really want to…"

Ironmouth the Giant shrugged his shoulders and sighed a giant sigh. "You don't have a choice. This afternoon, Princess Rose is due to take a stroll in the forest. Capture her and bring her back here!"

"As you wish, Dad…" sighed Little Giant.

"What luck!" gasped Scatterbrain. He could rescue Princess Rose quite easily from the little giant, and bring her back to live at Luckless Castle.

He realised he would need another horse for the princess to ride. This time he didn't want to make any mistakes. He rushed back to the village, bought a beautiful white horse for the princess and returned to the forest.

Scatterbrain shook with fear as he watched Ironmouth breaking tree trunks with his bare hands. He hoped Little Giant would be easier to defeat!

CHAPTER 5
Princess Rose

Suddenly, Scatterbrain heard ear-splitting screams.

"Let me go! Can't you hear me, you monster? Let me go or I'll get angry!"

He watched as Little Giant dropped the girl

he was holding over his shoulder onto the

ground. With her rose-pink dress and pink

ribbons it had to be Princess Rose!

Her cheeks were rosy too! She was so

beautiful that Scatterbrain fell in love with

her at once. He was even more determined

to rescue her!

Little Giant was much bigger and stronger than Scatterbrain but the brave knight felt full of courage. He ran up to Little Giant with a hand over his sword and shouted: "My name is Sir Scatterbrain, son of King Humphrey, and Prince of Luckless Castle. I have come to rescue Princess Rose. I shall show no mercy to whoever gets in the way!"

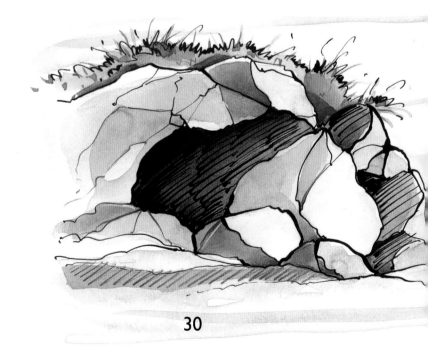

Princess Rose opened her eyes wide at the sight of Sir Scatterbrain and immediately fell in love with the brave knight.

"Let her go now!" the knight ordered.

"OK!" Little Giant whimpered. "She's yours!"

"Pardon?" Scatterbrain said, sounding disappointed. "Don't you want to fight? Even just a little?"

"No, thank you. My dad wants me to become a scary giant, but I'd much rather spend my time in the forest. I just want to catch butterflies."

Scatterbrain looked confused. Could it be a trap? "If I were you, I'd leave before my dad gets here," Little Giant urged.

But it was too late! Ironmouth stood

in front of them, looking angry!

"Where do you think you're going?"

He bent over Little Giant, who tried to look

very little indeed.

"What will people think if they know we

are allowing prisoners to escape?"

He turned to Scatterbrain: "And what about you, little squirt? What do you think you'll fight me with?"

Sir Scatterbrain puffed out his chest. Being with the princess made him feel extra brave.

"With this!" he said, pulling his sword out of its scabbard.

For a few seconds, Ironmouth stared at the knight's weapon. Then his stomach swelled and he rolled around in fits of laughter.

The knight looked at his sword more carefully – it looked more like a duster! When saying goodbye to his nanny, Miss Jocelyn, he had put his sword down for a second next to the duster. He must have absent-mindedly picked it up instead of his sword!

The princess tapped the brave knight on his shoulder. "Why don't we run away now?" she urged.

"Yes, good idea!" he replied, and they ran to the clearing where the two horses were waiting. They galloped off into the forest as fast as they could.

"We will be at my castle soon, Princess Rose," Scatterbrain said over his shoulder, whilst holding on to the reins of her white horse. "I am so happy. I love you so much. Will you marry me?"

But the princess did not reply.

"I understand," Scatterbrain said. "You need time. You need to get to know me a bit more."

At the lime tree, he took the road to the village. When he was sure they were safe, he stopped and turned around to speak to his princess. But there was no princess! Only the white horse. He looked around, worried.

"Goodness me! What's happened?
Has someone kidnapped her
without me noticing?"
Then he heard a voice calling
in the distance. "Hello, hello, my
brave knight!"

Sir Scatterbrain saw Little Giant
running towards him with the
princess on his back.

"You went too quickly! The princess didn't get a chance to climb on her horse!" panted Little Giant. Sir Scatterbrain's face went red with shame! But the princess thought it was very funny. "Your plan was almost perfect, my dear knight!" she laughed.

"Right," Little Giant said. "I'd better go. I spotted two very nice butterflies on my way here. Don't forget anyone this time!"

He said goodbye and ran off in a flash.

A month later, Luckless Castle held the wedding reception of Sir Scatterbrain and Princess Rose. Sir Scatterbrain could not stop staring at his beautiful wife. He was so happy.

Later, during dinner, Scatterbrain told his father the story of Princess Rose's rescue.

"Ironmouth?" King Humphrey interrupted him. "Did you say the giant was called Ironmouth?"

"Yes, Father. His son told me only one knight before me had managed to rescue a princess from him."

King Humphrey looked shocked and Sir Scatterbrain guessed why.

"... Father, that knight, could it have be you?"

"It was, indeed! You could say that Ironmouth doesn't have much luck with the Scatterbrains! Just like you, I defeated him with my courage and...

My – my courage and..."

He paused, moved closer to his son and whispered:

"Did you say you pulled a duster out of your scabbard?"

"Yes, Father. How about you?"

With a wink, the king whispered:

"I used a wooden spoon."

Franklin Watts
First published in Great Britain in 2015 by
The Watts Publishing Group

© RAGEOT-EDITEUR Paris, 2010
First published in French as
Le Chevalier Têtenlère

Translation © Franklin Watts 2015
English text and adaptation by Fabrice
Blanchefort.

Series Editor: Melanie Palmer
Series Advisor: Catherine Glavina
Cover Designer: Cathryn Gilbert
Design Manager: Peter Scoulding

ISBN 978 1 4451 3722 3 (hbk)
ISBN 978 1 4451 3725 4 (pbk)
ISBN 978 1 4451 3723 0 (ebook)
ISBN 978 1 4451 3724 7 (library ebook)

Printed in China

Franklin Watts
An imprint of
Hachette Children's Group
Part of The Watts Publishing Group
Carmelite House
50 Victoria Embankment
London EC4Y 0DZ

An Hachette UK Company
www.hachette.co.uk

www.franklinwatts.co.uk

MIX
Paper from
responsible sources
FSC® C104740
FSC
www.fsc.org